Titanic Tears

Titanic Tears

Leaving Ireland

Ned W. Schillow

and

Dru T. Schillow

Copyright © 2007 by Ned W. Schillow and Dru T. Schillow.

ISBN: Hardcover   978-1-4257-8222-1
          Softcover   978-1-4257-8192-7

All rights reserved. No part of this book may be reproduced or transmitted in any form or by any means, electronic or mechanical, including photocopying, recording, or by any information storage and retrieval system, without permission in writing from the copyright owner.

This is a work of fiction. Names, characters, places and incidents either are the product of the author's imagination or are used fictitiously, and any resemblance to any actual persons, living or dead, events, or locales is entirely coincidental.

This book was printed in the United States of America.

To order additional copies of this book, contact:
Xlibris Corporation
1-888-795-4274
www.Xlibris.com
Orders@Xlibris.com
40630

DEDICATION

This book is dedicated
to all the immigrants
who were sailing to America
on the Titanic.

Sadly for many, their dreams did not come true.

Titanic Monument in Queenstown, Ireland (now Cobh)

Introduction

Lady Liberty, standing so proudly nearby, holding her torch of freedom as a symbol of welcome for the many boatloads of immigrants from Europe.

Ellis Island, teaming each day with hundreds upon hundreds of new arrivals who are talking nervously in dozens of different languages as they waited their turn with the officials.

Nurses and doctors examining the people for diseases, even using button hooks to check their eyes.

Dormitories, with 50 beds to a room, serving as the temporary quarters until the newcomers are sent on their way or returned to their old country.

Poor people, usually dressed in tattered clothes, clinging to their few belongings all wrapped up in a bedroll or lovingly tucked away in a battered suitcase. But in their thoughts danced a common dream—a dream of a new start in America.

12,000,000 people passing this way, finally moving on by foot or by horse drawn carriage or by train, ready to enter their new lives.

This is the story of two cousins, coming to America to make it their home.

Part I

1909

Chapter One

"Go on! He's not lookin'!" whispered the older boy.
"Are ya sure?" replied the younger of the two.
"I told ya I'd keep a look out for ya!"

Sean Monaghan, the younger of the two, reached down to dig another potato from the ground. He already had pulled out six of the spuds and had placed them in his burlap sack.

"Hurry up!" coaxed the older boy.

"Hey! What are you two doing?" shouted the landowner. The boys turned their heads toward the voice that was booming from the house. "Go on now. I know who you are! Get away from my potatoes!"

Sean raised his head, turned, and ran toward the other boy. They took off running towards the fence as fast as their legs would carry them. They could hear the farmer's dog barking in chase.

"I have told you boys before!" shouted the potato farmer. "Leave my crops alone, you no good hooligans!" The dog was getting closer. The boys could hear it snarling.

They leaped over the fence and tore across the field as fast as they could. Once they got far enough away from the farmer to where they felt safe, they stopped to catch their breath. The watchdog quieted down.

The older boy looked at Sean and started to smile. The smile grew into a grin, which caused Sean to grin, and finally their grins turned into laughter.

"Do ya think he knows it was us?" asked Sean.

"Nah, I don't think so," said the other.

The boys knew that the farmers had experienced problems with the potato crops in recent years. Fortunately, things were much better than they were during the potato famine sixty years earlier, but now even simple problems with the potato crop made everybody nervous. After all, nearly one quarter of all the people in Ireland left their country for America, trying to avoid starvation and poverty.

Even now, earning a living in Ireland was difficult, and people still were moving across the Atlantic. Money was not easy to come by, and the boys knew that times were tough for their mothers too, especially since their dads had both left Ireland about a year ago. Their fathers would send money home from America, but it never lasted long, so on occasion the boys would help themselves to some crops in the neighboring fields. They knew it was wrong, but it was better than starving.

"Come on, cousin," said the older boy to the other. "Let's get out of here!"

"Okay. Boy, that was a close one. Did ya see the teeth on that dog?" Sean picked up the burlap bag of potatoes, hoisted it over his shoulder, and they headed for home.

Sean was eleven, two years younger than his cousin, but the two of them were very close. After their fathers had traveled to Pennsylvania to seek a better life for their families, the boys had gotten even closer. Many of their aunts and uncles and other cousins still lived in their village, but these two were the closest by far. Sean really looked up to him, and sometimes he knew that what his cousin coaxed him into doing was wrong, but he went along with it anyway. The dare was fun, the plan was fun, and the execution of the plan was the best part, especially if they did not get caught.

Sean looked over at his cousin as they headed down the dirt path back to the village. "I hope the farmer did not know it was us." His red hair was in need of a brushing. His cousin tousled his head of hair.

"We will be fine!"

But they were not fine. Later that day there was a knock at Sean's door. His mother was busy preparing dinner.

"Now who could that be?" she said as she wiped her hands on the towel. She opened the door, and there stood the farmer. Sean could feel his throat tighten and his heart sink.

"Mrs. Monaghan," began the farmer. "Earlier today I saw your son and his cousin sneaking around my property and stealing potatoes from my field." His mother glanced at her son and then at the potatoes sitting on the counter in the kitchen. "Now I know that times are tough right now for ya, being that your husband is in America and all, but times are tough for all of us, and I need every potato in my field just to try to make some profit this year!"

"I must apologize for my son's actions," Mrs. Monaghan said. "He really is a good boy."

"Hrrumph!" snorted the farmer glaring at Sean. "Your son would not be doing this if his father was still here."

"Please, here are the potatoes back," she said. "I apologize for my son's actions, and he will be disciplined for this."

The farmer grabbed the sack of potatoes and said, "I should hope so!"

"Hey! That's my sack!" shouted Sean. The farmer just grinned and walked away, sack in hand, as his mother told him to hush up.

"The farmer was right," his mother began. "You would not be doing this stuff if your dad were here." Sean drifted off thinking about his dad as his mother continued to scold him. He really missed his father so much. He remembered trudging along the River Lee together, searching for wild game. He thought fondly of the time they spent working on the sheepfold, even though it seemed like such hard work at the time. Then there was the one time they traveled all the way into the city of Cork—such an adventure. All those shops and busy streets and the grand cathedral were amazing. They used to do so much together.

Sean's eyes filled with tears thinking about his dad so far away. Big tears. He missed him so much. Thank goodness he had his cousin to play with. He and his cousin were inseparable. They walked to school together each day. They played down by the stream a lot looking for fish, and they loved to run along the paths around the countryside. His cousin's younger sister, Kathleen, was always trying to play with them too, and the two boys had fun trying to leave her behind all the time and making her cry. Sean always felt bad when she finally broke down into tears, but she was a pain, and the boys did not want to be burdened with her all the time.

The last time the boys got caught in the potato field, Sean's father was still home. When the farmer came to the house, Sean's mother was really mad, but he was sure he saw a small grin on his dad's face at his potato prank. Later that night, his dad said, "Now son, what you did was wrong, but I suppose boys will be boys! Don't let it happen again."

Sean's dad really understood him, and his eyes welled up in tears again as he thought of his dad so far away.

On occasion the boys would help themselves to some crops in the neighboring fields

Chapter Two

Michael O'Brien, Sean's cousin, was thirteen years old. Even though he was two years older than Sean, he enjoyed spending time with his younger cousin. Sporting dark brown hair and bright green eyes, Michael was much taller than Sean and was very slim. "So what should we do today?" he asked his cousin.

"I don't know, but we better not get in trouble. My mom is still mad about the potatoes."

"Yeah, my mom is too," said Michael. "Hey, let's go play down by the stream."

"Can I come too?" asked Kathleen. The two boys rolled their eyes at each other. Then Michael grinned at Sean and winked. He looked at his sister and said, "Sure. Come with us." Sean did not know what was in store for his little cousin Kathleen, but Michael was coming up with some scheme for sure. Kathleen was thrilled with the invitation.

Michael always was the schemer. It was Michael's idea to take the potatoes both times! Michael was the one who came up with the idea to scare old lady McIntire by tapping on her windows late at night, and it was Michael's idea to skip school and go into Mr. O'Neill's pasture and tease the bull. That was probably Michael's worst idea ever. Sean could still see his cousin rubbing his rump all the way home after the bull gave him a firm head-butt right into his backside!

Michael's dad had joined Sean's dad when they went to America to find work and make their fortune. The plan was that eventually they would bring their families across the Atlantic to New York City, where they could board a train for Philadelphia, and then travel to their new home in Norristown, Pennsylvania. Sean's dad had found a good job at one of the local iron works, but Michael's dad had not been so lucky. He was working part-time on the loading docks at the *Times Herald*, the local newspaper, and sometimes picked up odd jobs working for the railroad. Oh, Michael's dad was still sending home some money, but not as much as Sean's dad was able to do. Since they were family and lived close to each other, their mothers would often pull the money together and get things for both households as needed.

"Hey, hang on!" said Kathleen.

"Hurry up! You are so slow!" Michael shouted back to his sister. Kathleen picked up the pace to catch up to the boys.

Soon they were all down by the stream. The boys busied themselves turning over rocks and looking for anything that scampered away. Kathleen sat on the edge of the water watching the two boys play in the stream.

"Hey look! There's a snake!"

"Where?" shouted Kathleen. "I want to see it." Michael winked at Sean and grinned.

"Yeah, it's a big one too!" shouted Sean. Kathleen edged her way down to the bank of the water. Michael moved out of the way. She leaned in to take a closer look as Michael came up behind her and pushed her into the water. Kathleen lost her balance, and down she went into the icy stream.

"That's not funny!" she shouted as she started to cry. Kathleen was soaked from head to toe.

"You know there are no snakes in Ireland!" Michael added as Kathleen ran home, crying.

"You're going to get it!" was the last thing they heard her say as she disappeared over the hillside. The two boys continued to laugh as they put their shoes back on, preparing to go back home where they knew they would get another earful from their mothers.

Fortunately this time their mothers, who were on their way to the market in town, were not as upset as the boys thought they would be. But they did warn them not to pick on Kathleen, and the boys promised that they would not do it again. Kathleen stared angrily at her mean brother and cousin from behind her mother's dress. She stuck her tongue out at her brother, who responded by giving her an evil look. The boys left their mothers' presence and headed behind the nearby barn.

"Hey, let's go into town and see what's going on today. Race ya!"

Sean and Michael sprinted into town. Michael was by far the faster runner of the two and had already caught his breath when Sean finally caught up to him. The two boys walked into the market area of town, chatting away about how funny Kathleen's face was when she got out of the water.

"Remember that time we took Kathleen to the cemetery and told her ghost stories?" said Sean.

"Yeah, she sure was scared!" replied Michael. The boys sniggered at the memory of that day.

As the boys got closer to the market, Michael came up with the next scheme of the day. "Hey," he said, "the market is pretty crowded today."

"And?" asked Sean.

"Well, we may be able to help ourselves to some fruit to take home to our mothers."

"Have you forgotten about the potatoes already?" asked Sean. "Our mothers certainly remember it, and they'll tan our hides if we get caught."

"We won't get caught because the crowds are so big on market day. Come on, we'll be fine!" Michael tried to say reassuringly.

But the idea was not to pan out. When the boys got closer to the market, they not only saw their mothers chatting away at the fruit stand, but the potato farmer had spotted them the minute they arrived, and he was keeping a watchful eye on their antics. Sean was relieved that Michael did not want to try to nab some fruit anyway.

"Are you boys behaving yourselves?" asked Michael's mother.

"Yes," came the response in unison.

"Hmm," said Sean's mother, "I find that a wee bit hard to believe!" The two sisters smiled down at their sons.

"Come on, let's get outta here!" said Michael, and the two boys headed out of the village to explore other things. As they walked back down the street, the road got even more crowded with people making their purchases and hurrying home with their market goods. Michael said, "I wish you were my brother instead of my being stuck with Kathleen for a sister."

Sean beamed from ear to ear. "Yeah, you'd be a terrific big brother to have!"

Michael jumped up on a rock and recited an old Irish saying he had learned a long time ago.

> "Here's to you, and here's to me.
> Friends forever we will be.
> And if we should ever disagree,
> Then heck with you, and here's to me!"

He jumped down from the rock and wrestled his cousin to the ground as the boys laughed and repeated, "Then heck with you and here's to me!"

Chapter Three

"The teacher sure was not happy with you in school today," said Sean to his cousin.

"Yeah, and I have to show this note to my mother when I get home." Actually, the older boy was not very worried about the note at all. He didn't care very much about doing well in school, figuring he would be looking for work in a few years. He knew he didn't need very much education to work on one of the farms as a sheepherder or to dig out peat in the nearby bogs. Besides, he was counting on the fact that he would be leaving for America soon, where he could get a great job and make lots of money.

Kathleen looked at her older brother. "And not one word from you before I tell Mom," he added.

"I won't say anything. I promise," Kathleen said. Her little legs were making double time just to keep up with the boys.

As Sean headed over the last hill on their journey home from school with his cousin and Kathleen, he saw his mother and aunt waving excitedly from the front door of the house. "What do you think that is all about?" said Sean.

The three children began to run towards the home to see what all the commotion was about. "I hope it's not bad news," said Sean.

"A letter from your father!" Sean's mother said. "It just arrived." She began to rip it open to read its contents.

"What does it say? What does it say?" Sean repeated. His mother clutched the letter to her heart.

"He is sending for us!" she said as she began to read the exciting words of his letter.

My Dear Family,

  I miss all of you so much, but writing this letter makes me feel closer to you already. The time has finally arrived for the two of you to come to America! My job at the steel plant has really picked up. We just got a huge order for rail to be made for the Philadelphia & Western Railroad. Right now it connects Philadelphia to Strafford, but it is going to be extended to Villanova and connected to Norristown by 1912. And with my regular income along with the $200 I have already saved, you can now join me, my dear family.

  Maeve, carefully think about the few things you can bring with you and then sell everything else. While things are going well here, we can still use the extra money. And Sean, I'm depending on you to help your mother. You have much to pack and much to sell in the village, and she is going to need all the help you can give her. After all, you will be sailing in just three weeks. The vouchers for your ocean passage on the Lusitania will be sent to you shortly.

  I love you both and cannot wait until I can hug both of you over here on American soil. I know you are going to enjoy living here in Norristown.

Your loving husband and father,
Seamus

  Sean never thought that this day would arrive. His father had finally saved enough money and was now able to bring his mother and him to their new home. "I am going to America!" He jumped up and down as his cousin just stood by him and smiled. Kathleen was jumping up and down too. How excited Sean was to think that he would soon see his father again.

  "How are you going to get there?" asked Sean's aunt of her sister.

  "Well, the letter said that we will have to sell anything that we can't take with us, and that extra money will help us when we arrive in America. My husband has gotten tickets for us to take a ship called the Lusitania to New York. We will board this ship in Queenstown."

  "Queenstown?" Sean said. Except for that one trip to Cork, he had never been much further than his own village. This was going to be a huge adventure for him.

  "I am sure that Uncle Liam will be able to take us by cart to Queenstown where we will board the Lusitania," Sean's mother continued.

  "I wonder if it is a nice ship?" Michael's mother asked.

Sean was ecstatic with the news. He looked at his cousin and grabbed his shoulders. "I am going to America!" A new home. A new adventure. To be with his dad again.

Tears of joy ran down Sean's face. Happy tears!

I am sure that Uncle Liam will be able to take us by cart to Queenstown.

Chapter Four

Michael was not as excited by the news as his cousin was. He was sad inside, but he smiled and patted his cousin on the back. "You are going to America!" Michael tried to smile and put up a good front, but he was going to miss his best friend. He did not want Sean to go to America, at least not without him. Inwardly, Michael was even a bit jealous that his dad had not sent for them yet.

"Did we get a letter too?" asked Michael of his mother.

"No, son, not today," she replied. Michael hung his head as his cousin twirled around shouting, "I am going to America! America! America!"

"Do you think the roads are really paved in gold?" Kathleen asked innocently.

"Don't be silly," said her brother. "If they were, people would steal them."

"That's stupid," said his sister. "You can't steal a road!"

The group went into the house to start planning for the emigration to America. All except Michael that is. He was not in a festive mood. He turned and walked back over the hill just to be alone and to think. As he took a seat on a jagged rock near the old fence, he began to wonder if his dad would ever send for him.

Then his thoughts drifted towards the future when his cousin would be gone, and he'd still be stuck in Ireland without him. What would he do without his cousin? He thought of Kathleen. "Ugh! I'd have to play with her?" That thought did not thrill Michael one bit. He knew there was nothing that could be done. His cousin Sean would be leaving for America soon. Michael would just hope and pray that his own father would soon have the money to send for his family as well.

Michael stood up and kicked the dirt with his foot. "It's not fair. It's just not fair!" he repeated. He gathered his schoolbooks and headed back down the hill towards their homes. The letter from his teacher fell to the ground.

As he approached the houses, Sean was out front looking for him. "Where did you go?" he asked.

"I had some things to do," Michael lied. Sean could tell something was wrong.

"Are you worried about that note from your teacher?" he asked.

"No, it's not that," Michael replied.

"Then what is it?"

"I don't want you to go!" blurted Michael.

Sean could see that Michael was hurt by the news. He patted his cousin on the back. "Hey, I am sure you will be joining us soon in America!" he added.

"Come on, Michael," teased Sean as he nudged his cousin in the side. "Remember: Friends forever we will be!"

"I guess," Michael replied. He looked at his cousin who still had a big smile on his face. Michael began to smile, and then he grabbed his cousin's shoulders and shouted, "You are going to America!" The boys began to jump up and down together.

The Monaghans lived simple lives, and Sean did not realize just how little they had.

Chapter Five

During the next few weeks the Monaghan family was very busy packing up their belongings. Sean realized that he was limited as to how much he was going to be permitted to take on the ship, but his mother reassured him that many of the things he was giving up would be replaced by nicer things when they got to America. Still, it was hard for Sean to say farewell to some of his toys and personal things. Most of his clothing would go with them in the steamer trunk, but toys and books and what little furniture they had would not be making the trip across the Atlantic Ocean. His mother did tell Sean that he would be allowed to take his favorite toy and book along on the trip, which pleased Sean greatly.

The furniture and kitchenware would be sold to the folks in the village, and even though they would not get a lot of money for their belongings, it would still help them to furnish their home in Pennsylvania. Sean tried to stay clear of his mother as she dashed frantically about the house because she seemed a bit frazzled by all that needed to get done before they left with Uncle Liam on the cart trip to Queenstown.

The Monaghans lived simple lives, and Sean did not realize just how little they had until they began to sort through it. The kitchen had a few pots and pans, plates, earthen crocks and a wooden table with four chairs. They had beds, of course, and two chairs and a bench by the fireplace, but other than that, there was not much else to part with. But as his father had always said, "The world cannot make a race horse out of a donkey," and so they had been content with what they owned.

"America is the land of opportunity," Sean's mother said. "We will furnish our new home with nicer things. Your father already has some things there for us. Isn't this all so exciting?"

Sean smiled at his mother. He was excited about this trip, but the closer it came to the day of departure, the sadder he became. Ireland had been his home for eleven years. He knew nothing but his village and his family there. What would his new home be like? What will the new village called Norristown be like? Would he make new friends? Who would he play with? How long would it be 'til Michael will be able to join him in America? So many questions went through Sean's head during the final few days that he would spend in Ireland.

Almost too quickly the day arrived for Sean and his mother to leave. They had sold the beds and linens, the kitchenware, the tables and chairs, and some oil lamps. Their small steamer trunk was packed with clothing, some blankets, and the Irish lace tablecloth. Yes, they were ready to go. Uncle Liam was tending to the horse while Michael and Sean carried out the trunk to the back of the cart. The horse whinnied at the commotion.

Many of the neighbors had come out to say their farewells, and all the relatives who Sean would be leaving behind were there. It was so hard to say goodbye to his friends and family, especially his cousin.

Tears of sadness filled his eyes.

"We better get a move on it before it gets dark," Uncle Liam announced. Sean looked at Michael. He wiped the tears from his face.

"Bye, Sean," said Kathleen. Sean glanced over at Kathleen and smiled and then turned back to his cousin.

"Ma," started Michael, "May I ride along with Uncle Liam to see Sean and Auntie off in Queenstown?" Michael's mother glanced at her brother.

"To tell ya the truth, I could use the company," Uncle Liam said. Michael smiled and looked back at his mother with pleading eyes.

"Okay, son, but you better behave!"

"This time I promise, and I mean it!" Michael said. Sean was excited that he did not have to say goodbye yet to his older cousin. And to be honest about it, this was the same reason that Michael was willing to go along on the cart ride to Queenstown; he just could not bear to say farewell yet either.

"Can I go too?" asked Kathleen. "Please!"

"Mom, no!" pleaded Michael. Michael's mom knew that her son needed some time with his cousin.

"No, honey, not this time," she said. Michael, relieved, smiled at his mother. "Michael, be good," she warned.

The boys hopped in the back of the cart while Sean's mother climbed up front with Uncle Liam. He grabbed the reigns and got the horse moving. Shouts of "farewell", "goodbye", "good luck", and "may the road rise with you" filled the air.

Sean waved goodbye to them all, and tears filled his eyes as his village disappeared over the hill.

That may be the last time you see your old home!

Chapter Six

Michael O'Brien and his cousin Sean settled into the back of the cart after the village vanished from sight. Michael said, "That may be the last time you see your old home!" His cousin looked at him and smiled, but inwardly he was actually feeling a bit homesick already.

Of course he knew he would miss his neighbors and friends, but now, as he looked back at their old cottage, he realized how much he would miss everything. Sean started thinking about the great rock by the swimming hole on the River Lee. He pictured the old road sign in the center of town, half falling over and badly in need of paint. He recalled little details from the potato field, and suddenly even the tree in the corner of the field was something he would miss. And, oh, would he ever again see so many shades of green as they appeared on the hillsides above his home?

He was not sure what life would be like in America for him. But he could hardly wait to see his father again. Sean continued to view the landscape of Ireland as they rode along. He wanted to remember as much of his homeland as he could. Tears of homesickness welled up in his eyes, but he soon cheered up with his cousin nudging him in the side.

The horse clomped along the path, and the cart bounced up and down in the ruts of the dirt road as they continued towards Queenstown. The boys chatted along the way, dangling their legs from the rear of the cart. They shared many stories, thinking about the things they had done in the past, the pranks they had pulled on Kathleen, the time spent together down by the stream and in the woods, and all the family gatherings they had enjoyed over the years, celebrating Christmas, St. Patrick's Day, birthdays and so much more.

After passing through some other small towns on the way and making their way along the outskirts of Cork, the cart soon reached Queenstown. "Here we are!" shouted Uncle Liam when they finally entered Queenstown. The boys spun around to catch their first glimpse of the town.

Queenstown was nestled on the steep slopes of Great Island, situated along Cork Harbor. Grand St. Colman's Cathedral stood proudly on the top of the hill overlooking the city, which was alive with activity. They all took notice of The Bench, where a number of elderly sailors met every day to relive their memories of the sea. What a fine view they had of the wide-open harbor from this spot. Uncle Liam managed to point out Lynch's Quay to the boys as well as the old town hall just before the grandest site of all appeared.

There she was: the Lusitania, moored out in the open waters. The Lusitania was one of the largest, fastest, and most powerful steamers sailing in the North Atlantic. With her four funnels, she looked so magnificent. In fact, Lusitania was the first British ship to have four stacks. The ship was 750 feet long, weighed 32,000 tons and was capable of traveling at 26 knots.

The ship was built by John Brown & Co. Ltd. in Glasgow and was launched on June 7, 1906. It could accommodate about 550 first class passengers, 450 second class passengers, and 1,100 third class passengers. The Lusitania was considered one of the finest ships afloat at the time, but Sean did not know any of this. He just knew that the ship was big! Really big!

As the boys unloaded the trunk and two small suitcases from the back of the cart, Uncle Liam helped his sister down from the cart seat, and they talked about the trip on which she was about to embark.

Michael's cousin looked at him and said, "I am going to miss you." He held out his hand to his cousin to shake it. Because he was older and trying to hide the tears that he felt forming in his eyes, Michael smacked his cousin's hand away, laughing at his antic. Then he said,

> "Here's to you, and here's to me.
> Friends forever we will be.
> And if we should ever disagree,
> Then heck with you, and here's to me!"

Both boys laughed again. Just then the Lusitania's mighty horn blew, and Michael could not get over how loud it was. Uncle Liam kissed his sister goodbye and gave his nephew a long hug. Then he looked at them both as if he was memorizing their faces, and softly he repeated that famous Irish blessing:

"May the road rise to meet you,
May the wind always be at your back,
The sunshine warm upon your face,
The rain fall soft upon your fields, and until we meet again,
May God hold you in the hollow of His hand."

Sean and his mother said their goodbyes and gathered up their belongings. Quickly they climbed into 'The Flying Fox', a tender that would take them out to the majestic ship. Soon the tender was loaded with mailbags and other passengers who were heading to America, and it started to chug away from the pier.

Michael and his Uncle Liam watched and waved goodbye from the docks as the tender sailed further and further away. They stood together and could just make out the passengers as they boarded the Lusitania, but it was very hard to distinguish one person from the other.

"There is Sean," shouted Michael. "I see him!" Uncle Liam stood silently by and lit his pipe. The smoke continued to bellow from the stacks of the Lusitania, and soon the mighty passenger vessel began to move. Michael convinced himself that he could see Sean waving from the decks, but he could not be certain. Together, Michael and his Uncle Liam stood and watched the Lusitania disappear from view. "May the rocks of your field be turned to gold," muttered Uncle Liam with a touch of sadness.

It was at this point that Michael finally let it all sink in. His best friend in the world had gone. He was off to America. Michael was now alone in Ireland. Uncle Liam tried to comfort him. He put his hand on Michael's shoulder and said, "Don't you worry. Your dad will be sending for you in no time." Michael was not so sure about that, but he did not say anything.

'Well, we best get back home," said Uncle Liam. Michael sadly put his hands in his pockets and turned toward the cart to return home.

The Lusitania was considered one of the finest ships afloat at the time, but Sean did not know any of this. He just knew that the ship was big! Really big!

Chapter Seven

Sean watched the coastline grow smaller and smaller as the mighty Lusitania began its journey to America. Thick black smoke bellowed from the smokestacks above. He convinced himself that he could see Michael standing with his Uncle Liam on the docks, but he could not be certain. As Ireland disappeared below the horizon, he could feel tears of homesickness welling up in his eyes. He would soon be seeing his father, and his mother was with him, yet so many memories seemed to be vanishing with that last glimpse of the Emerald Isle.

He wondered if he would make new friends easily in America. What would this Norristown be like? Was it bigger than his village in Ireland or smaller? Would his new house be a thatched cottage like the one they just left behind? Would there be a stream nearby to play in? What would his new school be like? Thoughts raced around in his head as the ship continued its journey westward.

Just then his mother said, "Sean, look!" She was pointing down the side of the ship. There were harbor porpoises leaping out of the water alongside the ship. He had never seen porpoises before, and he and his mom watched them until they stopped following along the ship's path.

He lifted his hands from the railing on the deck and returned to the third class accommodations that would be his temporary home for the next week. His cabin was small, but actually he thought it was quite nice. In fact, Sean even thought to himself that in some ways his cabin was even nicer than his home back in Ireland. The walls were freshly painted white, and they even had a steel basin to use at the far end of the room, positioned between the two bunk beds. He noticed the word "Cunard", the name of company that owned the ship, embroidered on each bedspread. The room smelled clean. Oh, not that his mother was a bad housekeeper, but their home in Ireland always smelled earthy, musty, and the thatched roof always gave off a slight odor.

The Lusitania was huge, and he had a lot of exploring to do. The adventure of being at sea helped to lift his spirits a bit. The more Sean explored the ship, the more he liked it. The Lusitania offered many third class passengers a five-day journey in a style that most of them did not experience back home. The first thing that he checked out was the third class dining room. This room was decorated with polished pine and had seating for over 350 passengers who sat at long wooden tables. There was even a piano at one end of this huge room. He also poked his head into the third class smoking room. He thought this was a very impressive room. He could only imagine what second and first class looked like on the decks above him, but third class passengers were not permitted to tour the other parts of the ship.

Sean ran back to find his mother who was not looking too well. In fact, her skin looked a shade of green. "What is wrong?" he asked.

"I think I am just not getting used to this sea travel," his mother said. Sean had no problem with the gentle sway of the ship, but his mother grew greener and greener by the second. Suddenly she stood, covered her mouth, and ran for the ladies' room. He knew that this would be a tough trip for her.

By this time, many of the people leaving Europe on these northern sea routes were from Austria-Hungary or Russia, and they were looking for factory jobs. Others were Jewish people from scattered places on the European continent, with plans to live in New York City. On the Lusitania, there were still many Irish people looking to start a new life—but certainly not by farming in the fields. Those days of harvesting potatoes or raising sheep under the orders of a landlord was something they were eager to never do again.

As each day passed on board the Lusitania, he met many other children his age who were also heading to America. One of the older boys Sean met was named Michael Finnegan, and he was going to a place called Wilkes-Barre, Pennsylvania. His entire family would be joining their uncle and auntie who already lived there and worked for one of the large coal companies. The open strip mines would provide them with steady work, which they never had in the peat bogs of Ireland. "Besides," said Michael, "I hear that there might even be some openings at the coal breakers, which would be even more exciting work!"

"Is Wilkes-Barre near Norristown?" Sean asked, but the other boy did not know. "I hope it is." He was hoping they would still get to see each other and remain friends once they disembarked from the ship.

He also met a girl named Katy O'Hara. She was going to a place called Buffalo. Sean laughed. "I think you are mistaken. A buffalo is an animal."

"It is also a town in New York," Katy said as she turned up her freckled nose and walked away. Michael Finnegan rolled his eyes while Sean laughed.

"You remind me of my cousin," Sean said.

There were many other people going to many other places that he had never heard of. Minnesota. Virginia. Massachusetts. And the list went on. The children passed time on board by playing games and racing around the third class deck space on board. The days on board the Lusitania seemed to fly by.

Sean and his new friend Michael even tried to sneak up to see what first class looked like, but their plans were quickly foiled by a steward who caught them before they had gotten a chance to explore.

"We may have to try that another time," said the Finnegan lad.

"If my cousin was here, we would have gotten upstairs with no problem at all," Sean declared.

"I'll be watchin' ya!" said the steward. Both boys laughed as they headed back to the dining room to eat. Sean's mother had not eaten one bit of food the whole trip. She was unable to keep anything down with the roll of the ship on the waves, but Sean's appetite had grown on board the Lusitania.

"That is the salt air," said a fellow passenger. "It gives you a good appetite." And Sean sure could put the food away! Plenty of porridge or oatmeal at breakfast, along with eggs, curried veal, and even corned beef. And the dinners offered fine choices of roast beef or pork, fish or steak, and even fresh vegetables out there in the middle of the ocean! Amazing.

One day during the journey, Sean and Michael were out on the deck for a bit of fresh air when they overheard some of the sailors conversing.

"They are calling them the Olympic class ships!" said one of the crewmen.

"And they are gonna be bigger than our lovely Lusitania?" asked the other.

"Aye. A lot bigger," he said. "The first ship is under construction and almost done. She is called the Olympic. The next ship under way goes by the name Titanic. You know how those White Star Line folks are. All their ship names end in -ic." Both of the crewmen laughed as they finished with the ropes and walked away.

"Those ships are really gonna be bigger than this one?" the one crewmen repeated as they walked out of hearing range.

Sean looked at his new friend and said, "I can't believe that they could build a ship any bigger or nicer than this one."

"I agree," said the Finnegan boy. "This ship is HUGE!" He stretched his arms from side to side to represent the size of this vessel." A strong gust of wind and salty water caught the boys off guard, making their eyes tear.

"I don't understand how a ship so big and so heavy floats anyway," added Sean as he rubbed the tears from his eyes. "If I threw a piece of steel into the stream back home, it would sink!"

"I don't know how it floats either," said the other. "I am just glad it does." Both boys laughed at this comment.

He could only imagine what second and first class looked like on the decks above him.

Chapter Eight

Uncle Liam and his nephew rode home almost in complete silence. The only stop they made was in Cork, where Uncle Liam let Michael get his picture taken at a photographer's shop in an effort to cheer him up a bit. Normally such a special treat would have been very exciting since it was the first time he ever had his picture taken, but all Michael could do was think of Sean. The trip back to the village seemed to take forever, and he just wanted to get home. He needed some time alone.

Over the next few days, Michael would wake up and try to figure out what part of the Atlantic Ocean his cousin was now sailing upon. He knew that by the end of the week Sean would be in New York and then head to Philadelphia. Such funny names that town in America has: Norristown. Michael wondered if he would ever see the day when he could call Norristown his home too.

Michael felt lonely. He did not realize just how close he and Sean were until Sean was gone. At the beginning of the week he spent most of his free time just sitting on his bed remembering all the fun they used to have.

He remembered the time that they all went fishing, and Kathleen fell in. It was not funny at the time because she almost drowned, but they laughed about it afterwards.

Michael thought back about their potato prank and the bull episode. That memory still hurt a bit!

Michael remembered the time that he and Sean scooped up all this dirt and mixed it with water and made a creamy substance and tried to sell their dirt pies to passersby. They were really young at the time.

Then there was the spring when he and his cousin had collected all the buds off the bushes and flowers and had gathered them in buckets. There were no flowers that spring. Boy, were their mothers angry with them.

He thought back to the time when they had incredibly heavy rains for three days. His mother and Sean's mother warned them not to cross the stream just behind their homes, but they did it just the same. Crossing it was still fairly easy, and they did get to see the amazing flooding in the River Lee. But then they could not wade back across the stream and, oh, how worried their parents were, even though he and his cousin just thought of it as a great adventure.

He remembered the fun they had exploring around the old gunpowder mills on the north side of town. It was gritty and dirty and even a bit dangerous, but it was also exciting every time they went there. The company had shut down only a few years before, so it was still easy to find all kinds of unexpected treasures in the debris. He and Sean never could understand why their mothers were so worried about the occasional streaks of gunpowder that lined their pants when they crawled through the batch houses, where "green charge" had once been mixed.

Then there was the time Sean and Michael took Kathleen into the woods. They told her that there were monsters in the forest, and then they ran and hid from her and made noises. That sure frightened her, and they laughed all the way home 'til their fathers dealt with them afterwards. He recalled so many memories since his cousin left. Marvelous memories. Mischievous memories.

As he sat on the edge of his bed staring at the wall, he fully realized just how lonely he was, and his cousin had only been gone for three days. He hoped it would not be long until his own father would send for him.

"Norristown," he repeated to himself. "Such a funny name!"

Sean couldn't tear his eyes away from this wonderful sight.

Chapter Nine

On the morning of the fifth day, Sean and his mother found themselves looking at the skyline of New York. The first thing they saw was the Statue of Liberty. The ship passed close by, and Sean couldn't tear his eyes away from this wonderful sight.

France presented the statue to the United States in 1886, but they had called it *Liberty Enlightening the World*. She stood proudly upon a tall, stone pedestal, with her right arm raised high in the air, holding a torch. Atop her head sat a seven-pointed crown to remind everybody of the seven seas. And, oh, how large she was! Her index finger alone was eight feet long!

In her left arm she clasped a huge tablet. Because of its angle to the ship, Sean struggled to read what was written on it. What he thought he saw was "JULY IV MDCCLXXVI," but he couldn't figure out what those strange words meant, since he had never seen Roman numerals before. Only after he was in America the next summer did he learn about July 4, 1776. His mother explained to him that the statue was made of copper, which had turned green over the years, but Sean didn't care. He thought the statue was the most beautiful thing he had ever seen.

As they passed the statue, the ship was clearly slowing down, and soon it was docked in New York harbor. However, to Sean's surprise, as the crowd of third class passengers left the Lusitania, they were immediately put on barges and taken out to nearby Ellis Island. He thought the building there was a grand looking place from the outside. But as they left the barge, he was busier trying to get his final glimpse of the Statue of Liberty than his first view of the processing center that the immigrants were entering.

Suddenly, Sean and his mother were inside the building, ready to go through the immigration process to be allowed into the United States of America. The building was crammed full of all kinds of people speaking all kinds of languages, and it was a bit frightening. Occasionally he would catch a bit of conversation that he could understand and learned that some people had been here for two weeks already, waiting to pass their physical inspection.

Sean looked up at his mother in alarm and was relieved to see that she looked quite healthy and her color was back to normal, now that they were once again on land. Even though he felt so grown up back home, he grasped her hand tightly as they approached the huge oaken table, where two officials sat, looking very stern.

Sean's mother handed the immigration documents to them. They glanced through the papers quickly, barked out several simple questions about their names and where they were heading. As soon as his mother said, "Norristown, Pennsylvania," they banged two large stamps onto the inkpads and then onto the documents and pointed to the next hall they were to enter.

Now they were in a large room, and clearly it was the doctors and nurses who were in charge here. Sean watched most of the people in front of them directed down to the next large hallway, but occasionally somebody would be pulled aside and ordered into a small, adjacent waiting room. People gasped and cried whenever this happened, so Sean knew that this was certainly not what he wanted to occur to them. What if he and his mother would be separated?

Fortunately, the two of them must have looked just fine, for they received what seemed like a simple six-second glance. They were then ordered towards the next hallway, which was clearly the direction for the healthy arrivals. But even now Sean did not think that he would ever set foot on American soil. He could see New York City. It was so close, yet he was still so far away. However, after only about four hours, the inspection and immigration procedures came to a close, and Sean and his mother were boarded on to a tender to take them into New York City.

Sean had never dreamed that New York would be so big! It was much bigger than Queenstown or Cork. As the tender docked, the newest inhabitants of America began to disembark. Sean's mother went down the gangplank first. She was glad to get back on solid ground again. Then Sean jumped from the steps, and he froze. He looked at his mom, and tears of joy ran down his face. "I am in America!" he said. His mother gave him a big hug.

"Yes, we are finally here," she added.

Over three million people lived here, nearly three quarters as many who lived in all of Ireland, and Sean felt like they saw nearly every one of them on their long walk to the train station. So many glorious sites to see. They would look down one street and actually see sheets hanging up to dry seven stories above the road below! Then a few streets later they would see many shops with wide glass windows full of the most fancy clothes and jewelry they had ever seen.

In fact, the streets were full of people in wonderful outfits: women in long, silken dresses and men in striped suits and celluloid collars. Amazing carriages passed them by, pulled by the largest, healthiest looking horses Sean had ever seen. Trolley cars clattered on tracks elevated above the streets.

When they passed by a beautiful hotel with a marble front, Sean begged his mother to let them go inside, for he could already glimpse the amazing interior. But she hushed him very quickly and moved him along. "After all," she said, "we are here with our everyday clothes and our steamer trunk and two beat up suitcases, tired, and looking a bit dirty from our long sea voyage. And there they are, rich Americans, feathers in their hats, dressed up in their finery, all very clean and clearly very rich. They would throw us out in a matter of seconds."

However, they still managed to have their small adventures. They purchased lunch from a sidewalk vendor. This was the first time Sean and his mother had ever tasted a hot dog, and it was such a warm, delicious treat as they bit into the soft roll and the juicy, brown meat.

Then Sean spotted post cards in a shop window and begged his mother to let him buy one to send to Michael. While she knew they had to be careful with their money, she also knew how important this was for Sean to do. He found one that he liked and addressed it to his cousin back in Ireland. The postcard had a picture of the Statue of Liberty on it. He wrote:

> *Dear Michael,*
> *How great it is here! We are in New York, and we saw the Statue of Liberty. Everybody is wearing the nicest clothing and the shop windows are full of so many wonderful things. But the streets are **not** paved with gold. It's just nonsense when people say that.*
> *Your cousin,*
> *Sean*

They mailed the post card, and then his mother said, "Now let's see about finding us the boarding house where your dad said we can spend the night."

Sean replied, "Mom. Why can't we just leave for Pennsylvania now?" Sean could not wait to see his father.

"Now Sean," said his mother, "I already told you that this would be a two day journey. It will soon be dusk, and we certainly don't want to keep traveling after dark. Besides, your father will not be meeting us at the train station in Philadelphia until tomorrow anyway."

"Aye," replied Sean. "But I can't wait!" His mother gave him a big hug, and they set off for the boarding house to spend the night.

They were immediately put on barges and taken out to nearby Ellis Island.

Chapter Ten

It had been nearly a week since Michael's cousin had left for America on the Lusitania. For Michael it had been one of the longest weeks of his life. He went down to the stream to play, but it was not any fun without Sean there. He was tempted to go back to the potato farm and take some more spuds, but without his lookout, it would be too risky. Michael walked into the market area in town but did not stay long because he did not have his best friend to joke with. Michael had other friends at school, but it was just not the same without his cousin.

"Do you want to play dolly with me?" his sister Kathleen said.

"No, I don't!" he snapped.

Michael's mother looked up from darning the socks and said, "Michael, ya can't keep moping around the house this way. You are gonna see your cousin again soon. Now let's see a smile on that face, and why don't ya do something with your sister."

Michael forced a smile and looked over at his sister. "Well, I guess we can do somethin', but I amn't gonna play dolly."

"Can we go down to the stream?" she asked.

"I suppose," was his response.

"Good!" said Kathleen. She put her doll back into its makeshift cot and put on her jacket. Michael grabbed his coat too and told his sister he would meet her outside.

Michael's thoughts again turned towards Sean. He looked over at the large tree at the end of the field and reminisced about the time he and his cousin had swatted a stick at the bee's nest. He laughed and said to himself, "That was a mistake!" He stuck his hands in his pockets and leaned against the wall near his home. "He probably forgot about me already. Hmm! Friends forever we will be! Yeah, sure."

As Kathleen walked out the door, their mother said, "And don't push your sister into the water!"

Chapter Eleven

Despite how exhausted he felt the day before, Sean still had trouble sleeping in the boarding house. There were all kinds of strange sounds all night, with the house creaking, people breathing heavily, and noise leaking in from the streets. Besides, he was so excited about seeing his father that his mind kept racing about all the things they would talk about. But morning finally came, and after a quick breakfast Sean and his mother were back on the streets, heading north with their luggage, going to the train station.

Sean had never been on a train before, and that adventure was as exciting for him as the trip across the Atlantic on the Lusitania. He sat down with his mother in their seat, and the conductor punched their tickets.

"All aboard!" the conductor shouted. With a lurch that made Sean's eyes grow huge, the train pulled out of the station.

"This train is heading to Philadelphia!" announced the conductor. Sean sat back and looked out the window watching the sights of New York grow smaller and smaller as they chugged away from the city. He enjoyed the scenery as they headed south through New Jersey. He had never traveled this fast before, and he liked to watch the scenery whiz by his window. The clickety-clack of the train along with its rocking motion made Sean very sleepy. In fact, he was soon fast asleep and slept most of the rest of the trip.

"Next stop, Philadelphia!" shouted the conductor.

"Come on, Sean, wake up," said his mother as she shook him.

Sean opened his eyes and stretched, "Where are we?" he asked.

"We are approaching Philadelphia now!" said his mother.

Sean sat up quickly, exclaiming, "I'll be seeing Dad soon!" He was more excited than ever. After all, they were now in the same state as his new home, which meant the journey was drawing to a close. He gazed out the window with great anticipation as the train traveled along the Delaware River, skirting along the edge of the surrounding marshlands, heading towards the city skyline. Sean was surprised to see that there was a man standing on top of the tallest building he could see. At that point he had no idea that it was a statue of William Penn, the founder of Pennsylvania.

As the train came to a stop, he was looking out at the faces in the station, but he did not see his father. They got off the train and headed into the station. That is when they saw him. There he stood with his hand waving, and he had a big grin on his face.

"Dad!" shouted Sean as he ran towards him. His dad already had his arms outstretched to greet him. Sean leaped into his open arms. It felt so good to be with his dad again, and soon Sean's mother joined the hug to complete a well-deserved family reunion. Sean's eyes were filled with tears of delight to see his father again.

"I have missed you both so much!" said Sean's dad as he kissed his wife on the cheek. "I am so glad you are finally here!"

They gathered the trunk of clothes and two small suitcases and headed out of the train station where Michael's dad was waiting with the wagon. Another round of hugs was extended to Michael's father.

"It is so good to see you, Uncle Patrick," said Sean.

"And it's good to see ya too," he replied. "When we get back to Norristown, I want to hear all about Michael and little Kathleen," he added.

"She is not so little any more!" said Sean's mother.

Patrick O'Brien replied, "Aye. I suppose she is not." He had a far away look in his eyes. He was glad that more of the family was now joining them in America, but deep down he really wished his wife and children were here as well. "In time," he thought to himself. "In time."

"How far is it to No-rus town?" said Sean.

"It is pronounced Norristown," corrected his father. "Well, we have a wee bit of traveling yet to do, so we better get crackin'!" As they pulled out of the station, Sean was surrounded by the new sights and sounds of Philadelphia. "This is where America started," said his father as Uncle Patrick nodded in agreement. "In fact, England once ruled over America just as they rule over Ireland now," he continued.

"Really?" said Sean.

"We're going to take you on a bit of a detour before we head to your new home," Sean's father told them as they headed east along Market Street. After a number of blocks they turned right onto Sixth Street, where there suddenly appeared a large brick building with a beautiful white tower. "That's Independence Hall," he continued. "That is where the capital of this country once was, and that is where the great patriots wrote the Constitution of the United States."

They circled around behind this stately building, and then as they turned right onto Chestnut Street, Sean's father continued to talk about the great leaders like Presidents George Washington and John Adams, who had lived here before the government moved to Washington D.C. A few blocks later he pointed to another smaller brick building and said, "That's Carpenter's Hall, where they wrote the Declaration of Independence, and that led to the Revolutionary War." These were all new words to Sean and his mother, and even his father admitted he still had much to learn about the history of their new land. But he finally said, "This is a wonderful land of freedom, and this is where it all began."

They continued on, making two more left turns through the old streets, and Sean learned a little bit about Benjamin Franklin as they passed by some buildings that Franklin had owned. He was a very famous Philadelphian who helped with the Declaration of Independence and the Constitution. But he had also been an inventor and a writer and a traveler. In fact, Sean's father knew that Franklin actually visited Ireland long ago. "When he saw the way the Irish were living under British rule, without enough money or food, he knew the colonies needed to do something drastic to get their freedom."

It was all so new and all so strange, but somehow it also was all so wonderful as they took in the sights. "America!" said Sean quietly to himself as the wagon headed out of Philadelphia, nicknamed The City of Brotherly Love.

After what seemed a very long ride, they approached Norristown at dusk. "Now ya won't have much time to explore today 'cause it's gettin' late, but tomorrow you will have a chance to check out your new neighborhood." Sean looked ahead to Norristown, his new home in America.

Since it was growing dark, they could not see much of their new home. But clearly it was much larger than their village back in Ireland. They crossed a large river called by a very strange name, the Schuylkill, as they entered Norristown. This made Sean quite happy, remembering the fun he always had in the River Lee. The brick buildings were much newer than most of the buildings in Cork, and he didn't see any cottages at all like their old home.

He noticed a few banks as they continued through the town, along with many shops. He spotted some churches with steeples so high they seemed to be poking at the moon. He noticed a large building with high columns and a round cone on top, which he soon learned was the courthouse. There would be so much to visit and so much to learn in his new town.

The wagon turned onto a small side street not far from the courthouse when his father said, "There it is. Your new home."

"And I am right across the street," said Uncle Patrick.

"Great!" said Sean. "It is nice to know that Michael will be close by when he gets here."

"Yep, and I am savin' more each day to get my family here too," announced Uncle Patrick.

"And now that I've gotten my family here, I may be able to give ya some help too," said Sean's father. "Family sticks together!" Patrick smiled as they pulled up to the house.

Sean saw some kids playing up the street that looked his age. That was encouraging. "I hope I make some new friends here," he thought to himself.

They made their way up the front path to the freshly painted, white door. The house was a row home, built of brick, and was at least two stories high. Sean couldn't be sure if there was a third floor or not, but then he spotted a small window high above the street. What a grand place this was compared to their old cottage.

Sean ran inside to check out his new home. As he entered the house, a staircase was directly in front of him. To the left was a living room, followed by a dining room, followed by a kitchen. To his amazement, there was a fine wood stove and a sink right there, inside the house.

He raced up the steps to find three more rooms that would be their bedrooms and a sewing room for his mother. Then he spotted another door. He opened it up and there was yet another stairwell. Curious, he continued up these stairs and soon learned that the small window he spotted from the road was actually for the attic. How wonderful all this would be.

After the excitement of seeing the new home, they all sat down to relax and to get acquainted again. Sean's father started by telling them about his job.

"I'm lucky to be working the day shift," he began, "because most of the new hires work there at night instead. Of course, working around the iron works is hot, but it's good honest work, and it pays well. Besides, with all the new rail that the subway and train lines are going to need, we don't have to worry about the plant shutting down." Sean asked if the work was dangerous, and his father admitted that it was. "But," he continued, "I'm not in the front areas where they pour the molten steel, so that makes things a lot safer for me. Maybe someday I will take ya to my work so you can see what I do."

"Okay," said Sean. He looked forward to spending as much time with his father as possible.

"Now tell me," interrupted Uncle Patrick. "I am dieing to know about Michael and Kathleen." So Sean and his mother filled in both men about the rest of the family back in faraway Ireland.

With all the news of home, they lost track of time, and it had gotten late. Patrick said his good nights, and Sean crawled into bed for his first night in his new home.

"That's Independence Hall," he continued.
"That is where the capital of this country once was."

Chapter Twelve

Sean's postcard and a letter from America both arrived in the mail on the same day for Michael. First he looked at the picture on the postcard and turned to his cousin's words on the back. Michael smiled as he read it. Then he picked up the letter that was from his father.

Michael quickly ripped open the envelope to see what his dad had to say. "Maybe he's sending for us now!" said Michael, as his mother joined him to read the contents of the letter.

> Dear Michael,
>
> This is a big "hello" from America. Your cousin Sean and your Aunt Maeve arrived a week ago and are getting settled in. They were really tired when they arrived here, but now they are fully rested and are beginning to get used to Norristown.
>
> You have no idea how much I miss you, son, and I love you so much. I'm still working hard, saving up money for you and your sister and your mother to come over here so we can be together again. But it isn't easy since I still haven't been able to find steady work. Your Uncle Seamus keeps his ears open for a job for me at the mill, but I never worked in a steel plant, and they prefer to hire experienced workers.
>
> Anyway, I have a new job working on the Norristown trolley that I told you about before. I still can't seem to get a full time job anywhere, but it is a bit of extra money, and I'm saving as much as I can. I love you and miss you—and I want to remind you to be the man of the house and take care of your mom and Kathleen.
>
> Remember, son, no matter how long the day, the evening still will come. We'll just have to wait a while, but someday we will all be together again.
>
> Love,
> Your Dad

Michael sat the letter on the table.

"I am never going to get to America!" he shouted as he ran angrily to his bedroom.

And so it seemed for a long, long time, because Michael and Sean ended up corresponding by letters for many, many months. What made it even worse was how slowly the mail traveled. With each letter that Michael wrote and posted at the local office, it might be several days before it would be sent on to the city post office in Cork. From there it would be sorted into bags and taken to the wharfs for passage to America.

A few days might pass before the mailbags would get loaded onto a ship for a weeklong voyage across the Atlantic. While it was true that the mail would then be sorted in mid-ocean, it still faced another delay when the bags were unloaded on the dock of New York. Finally they would be sorted again, sent to Philadelphia, and eventually to Norristown, where Sean would at last receive a much waited for message from Michael.

Then began the same, slow trip in reverse when Michael would send his reply to Sean. News certainly traveled slowly. But the people really did not mind. After all, these were precious notes from friends and families, and the new ships were making the exchange of mail faster than before, and slow news was better than no news at all.

It was true that the mail would then be sorted in mid-ocean.

Part II

1909-1912

Chapter Thirteen

Dear Michael,

    I have been in Norristown for a few weeks now. Your dad is doing really well, and you will like your house when you get here. It is made of brick. In fact, almost all the houses are brick here instead of stone like back home. Your house is across the street from mine. I have not made any friends yet.

    I miss doing things with you a lot.

    The first week I explored the nearby stream. There are a few salamanders but there are so many frogs that are really fun to catch. Those salamanders are exciting—about four inches long and really fast both on the land and in the water. You are going to like the stream and the way it winds through the woods. I sure hope to see you soon.

    School starts in two weeks. Then maybe I will meet someone our age to play with.

Your Cousin,
Sean

He noticed a few banks as they continued through
Norristown, along with many shops.

Dear Sean,

 I have not been to the stream near our village since you left, except for one day I took Kathleen down there. No, I did not throw her in if that is what you are thinking. It just is not the same in Ireland without you. I sure wish we could come to America soon.

 Kathleen is looking over my shoulder and bothering me, so I am going to end this letter and really let her have it!

Your cousin,
Michael

Chapter Fourteen

Dear Michael,

    Norristown is a lot bigger than our village, and there are so many people from so many different backgrounds. We live in one section of town near a few other families from Ireland, and not far from here there is an Italian section of town. Around the town there are many German-speaking people. It is hard to talk to some of them because they don't speak English, well, at least to me they don't.

    School starts tomorrow, so I must go to bed early. I am a bit nervous about going to school without you by my side.

    My dad said that the school here has more than one room. The classes are divided a bit by different ages, called grades. I am frettin' about tomorrow 'cause I don't know anyone. The post office is on my way to school, so I will post this letter then.

    How is your family?

Your cousin,
Sean

Dear Sean,

    I got your last letter. By now you are in school. I am too. It used to be fun when you were here. Remember the time we kept making bird noises and drove teacher crazy? She kept looking from one side of the room to the other 'til she figured out who it was. Our dads sure were not happy about that. How is Dad? Kathleen keeps pestering me to do things, like pretending to have tea parties and playing school. She is such a bother.

Your friend,
Michael

Chapter Fifteen

Dear Michael,
    Your dad is fine. My dad got hurt at work and is home right now, but he will be fine soon. He has a huge bruise on his leg from where a steel rail hit him at the plant, but he isn't limping at all any more and will start work again by Friday. How is Uncle Liam? How is your mom?
    I really don't like some of the kids in my school. They are kind of mean. They tend to stick to their own groups, and they pick on me being smaller than most of the kids in my class, and they say that I talk English funny. I don't think so. Do you?
    On the weekends, I help around the house and explore down by the stream. They call the stream a creek around here.
    I sure wish you were here to stop the kids at school from picking on me, you being so big and all.
    I learned that there is a holiday here in November called Thanksgiving. You just sit around and eat all day. I know you like to eat even though you are skinny as a branch. Are you still skinny?

                                                              Your cousin,
                                                                   Sean

Dear Sean,

Everyone is good here. I tried to take Kathleen with me to the potato farmer's field, but she is not a good look out like you or me. The angry farmer spotted us in no time, and I practically had to carry her to get out of there before he caught us. He did not come to Mom's house this time. Guess 'cause we left with nothin'.

My mom got a letter from Dad. He says that he has saved some more money to send for us soon. I hope so.

From,
Michael

Chapter Sixteen

Dear Michael,
 Happy New Year. We did something special today. We rode into Philadelphia and watched the Mummer's Parade. We had a great time listening to the banjos play and looking at their fine costumes. I hope you had a nice Christmas. I got some new clothes for school. Some of them even came from Chatlin's, which is a large shop here in Norristown. Only here they call it a department store, because it is so big and has many different sections or departments to buy things in. I also got a book about ships, which is fun to look at as it reminds me of our trip on the Lusitania. It gets cold in Norristown in the winter, so tell your mom to pack lots of warm clothing when you come to America.

Best Wishes,
Sean

Dear Sean,

    Sorry I have not written in a bit. I just got a bit lazy. I told Mom not to worry about packing warm clothes for the winter. My dad is never going to send for us, so I'm sending you a picture of myself so you don't forget what I look like. Uncle Liam had the photographer take this picture on the day you left for America.

    Happy St. Patrick's Day to ya. Kathleen says hello.

Your cousin,
Michael

Chapter Seventeen

Dear Michael,

    Spring is here, and it is almost time for Easter. A lot of trees are blooming here, and things are getting green, but it isn't like the greens in Ireland. But one thing that was great was our St. Patrick's Day parade! That's right! Even though we are so far away from Ireland, we had a parade with horses and horns and bands playing Irish music! A lot of people wore green! It sure was fun.

    Your dad has been fixing up his house and bringing in some more furniture. You should not give up. I think he is going to send for you all soon. I sure hope so. I want to explore America with you. I still don't have many friends at school.

    Tell Kathleen there are no streets paved in gold here.

    By the way. The squirrels here are grey. Not like the red ones back home.

                                                    Sincerely,
                                                       Sean

Hey Cousin,

School is now over for another year. I did better than last year. I suppose without you around I am studying a wee bit more than I used to.

Everyone in Ireland is talkin' 'bout those new ships they are building in Belfast. They are going to be big. Bigger than the Lusitania that took you away from here.

Kathleen and I drove Mom crazy last night. We pestered her to stay up later so we could finish a game of marbles. I won, of course, and it's a whole lot more fun than playing tea party!

Best Wishes,
Michael

Everyone in Ireland is talkin' 'bout those new ships
they are building in Belfast.

Chapter Eighteen

Dear Michael,

    I remember hearing about those big ships when I was on the Lusitania. They are White Star Line ships, and I think they are called the Olympic and the Titanic. I heard some of the crew talkin' about them. They said they were bigger but not faster than the Lusitania. Is it true?

    Thanks for the picture of yourself. I hung it up on the wall of my bedroom. What have you been up to?

Sincerely,
Sean

Dear Sean,

    You are right. The Olympic is already sailing the Atlantic, and the other one will be done soon too. Belfast and all of Ireland are proud of the ships we built.

    If I ever make it to America, maybe I will see these great ships as we pass them on the ocean. That would be a sight. Anyway, Kathleen and I built a little hidden house by the stream. We go there sometimes and talk. She is okay I guess. Suppose without you around I have gotten to know her better.

    I'd rather spend time with you then Kathleen, but she is okay, I guess. Are the squirrels really grey?

Your cousin,
Michael

The Olympic is already sailing the Atlantic, and the other one will be done soon too.

Chapter Nineteen

Dear Michael,
    How are you? I am okay. My mom has one of them colds. The leaves on the trees are pretty here in the autumn. Yellow, gold, red, brown, orange, green and more. It is like a dreamland when they all fall and fly around in the wind.
    How is everyone back home? I do miss you and Ireland. As pretty as the leaves are here, now, I do miss all the shades of green back home. I have made a few friends, but they will never replace you. It has been too long since I have seen you. Hope you are well.

Your cousin,
Sean

Dear Sean,

    We are all good here. Uncle Liam and Mom send their love. Tell my dad I said hello. Kathleen and I went to the market, and we talked the whole way there. Ya know, she isn't so bad, I suppose. She actually makes me laugh sometimes.

    The other day I taught her that saying. You know . . . .

> "Here's to you, and here's to me.
> Friends forever we will be.
> And if we should ever disagree,
> Then heck with you, and here's to me!"

    She could not get it right. She kept saying, "Then heck with you and heck with me!" Mom and I laughed 'til our sides hurt.

Your cousin,
Michael

Chapter Twenty

Dear Michael,

    My dad has given your dad some money to save to send for you, Kathleen, and your mom. Don't give up. It is going to happen. I know it is. It is hard to believe we've been here more than two years already.

    Guess what. My mom is going to have a baby! You are gonna be a cousin again. I hope it's not a girl. I don't want a little Kathleen hanging around with me.

    I missed a day of school to go back to Philadelphia with my dad to get some supplies we need. It is a long ride from Norristown to Philadelphia, but it was a fun day. We found all the things we needed, and then Dad surprised me by taking me to visit the new Wanamaker's store. It is a huge department store building that just opened, and it is 12 stories tall! We mostly just walked around, and the only thing we bought was a surprise to give to Mom. A fancy new blanket for the baby. I wanted us to buy a blue one because I really want it to be a boy, but Dad said we better just get a white one.

    I hope you are okay.

Regards,
Sean

Dear Sean,

 I told ya before that Kathleen is okay. If you have a sister, it won't be so bad once you get to know her. I mean I do wish you were my brother still, but as far as girls go, sisters can be okay. I told my mom about your mom having a baby. She is all excited about it.

 Mom got a letter from Dad, but she is not home, so I don't know what it says. I am posting this one now 'cause I am going to the village to chase the cats in the market.

Your cousin,
Michael

I missed a day of school to go back to Philadelphia with my dad to get some supplies we need.

Part III

1912

Chapter Twenty-One

Sean was playing down by the creek near his home when something strange caught his eye. It was gazing back at him. He froze. It froze. He blinked. It stared. He did not know what to do. He had never seen one before. It started to move from the rock. He slowly stepped back. It moved so strangely. He could not take his eyes off of it. It kept a close eye on him. What would it do next? Would it attack? Was it poisonous? Could he approach it?

Then the pronged tongue slithered from its scaly mouth, and it started to wiggle from the rock and into the water straight toward him. Sean's eyes grew wide as he scrambled up the loose rocks and stood on the bank of the creek, but by then the snake was gone.

"Wow. A snake!" Sean said. "Michael would love to see one of them!" Sean thought about the story that explained how St. Patrick chased all the snakes out of Ireland. The legend said that he drove them into the sea by banging on a big drum made of snakeskin. The noise was so loud that the snakes couldn't stand it. But since they had no hands to cover their ears, all they could do was to try to slither away. As they kept moving, the story goes, St. Patrick kept moving as well, banging louder and louder on the drum, until they finally escaped into the Irish Sea where they all drowned.

Of course, some people say he chased them away by ringing church bells. And other people say he had to fool the last, big snake into a small trunk. Sean suspected the stories were all a bit of nonsense, but who knows? After all, there really are no snakes in all of Ireland.

Sean took off for home as fast as he could. He could not wait to get that pen and paper ready and write to his cousin about the snake he had just seen. They had often talked about what snakes must be like since neither had actually ever seen one in Ireland, but now Sean could tell Michael just what they look like and how they move. He raced home to share his story while it was fresh in his memory. "A snake," he said to himself as he tore through the woods towards his street.

Sean ran into the house. His mother was fanning herself in the rocker. "Mom! Mom! Guess what I saw down by the stream?"

"Hold on there," she said. "You got a letter from your cousin. I think you should read it first before you tell me about your latest adventure."

Sean spotted the letter on the table and picked it up. He opened it. He read it out loud.

> *Dear Sean,*
>
> *I am coming to America! Dad finally saved enough money for us to make the trip. I am finally going to see you again. Isn't this great? We will be coming over in April. And here is the best part. We will be traveling on the Titanic! The largest ship ever built in the world! An Irish built ship! I am going to be seeing you soon. We board in Queenstown just like you did. There is so much to do before we get there, so I am going to start packing now.*
>
> *Sean, it will be great to see you again.*
>
> *Your cousin and friend,*
> *Michael*

Sean looked up from his letter. His mother was smiling from ear to ear. Her belly was now showing the baby, and she rubbed it while she spoke.

"For real?" Sean asked.

"Aye, so it is. I knew about it several weeks ago, Sean, but your uncle and your dad and I thought you'd like to hear the news from Michael. Are ya happy?"

"Happy? I am thrilled!" said Sean. I can't wait 'til he gets here. We will have to throw a party for the O'Briens when they arrive." He wore a huge smile on his face as he waved the letter in the air.

"That's a great idea," his mother said. "We will throw them a good ole' fashioned welcome party.

Sean's cousin would be here soon. And he'd be coming on the Titanic, the ship he heard the crew talking about when he sailed to America. An Irish ship. How lucky his cousin was to be on that ship. There had been some articles in the local paper about these new ships, and Sean knew that the Titanic was the largest ship in the world. Sean felt a little jealous that his cousin would arrive on a ship nicer and bigger than the one that brought him here, but the Lusitania was faster, and that was a special thing to brag about if he needed to when Michael arrived in Norristown.

"I can't wait to see him," Sean said as he ran out of the house and across the street to his uncle's home. He wanted to hug his uncle and thank him for finally bringing his best friend in the world over to America. Tears of joy streamed down his face.

Sean had forgotten all about the snake.

We will be traveling on the Titanic! The largest ship ever built in the world!

Chapter Twenty-Two

The cold winter days began to mellow, and the light of day lasted longer each evening. Spring was finally here. Many of the daffodils were in bloom, and the robins had returned to hunt for worms. It was early April when Sean received the next letter from his cousin.

Dear Sean,

We will be leaving on the Titanic around April 10th. I am so looking forward to seeing you and Dad again. Kathleen has been as excited as I am. She still thinks she is going to see golden roads when we get to America. I think she will be disappointed. I have been reading a lot about the Titanic lately. Titanic is the largest man-made moveable object ever built.

Some of the newspapers call Titanic "The Wonder Ship". It has a swimming pool, restaurants, and even a gym. I think it is going to be a grand trip.

Can you believe that you and I will be together again? Here's to you and here's to me. Friends forever we will be. Ha, ha.

Oh, I forgot to mention that the Titanic is a wee bit heavier than her sister ship, the Olympic. That is why they say Titanic is the largest ship in the world. There are millions of rivets in her holding her together, and they say she is unsinkable. She has watertight compartments that keep the water out I guess.

I can't wait to see you.

Your cousin,
Michael

Sean showed the letter to his mother. "He leaves April tenth." He walked over to the calendar to check today's date. His eyes grew wide. "He is leaving

Ireland today!" He began to jump up and down as tears of excitement welled up in his eyes. "When was that letter postmarked?"

His mother looked at the envelope. "It was written back in early March. I wonder why this letter took so long to get here?" she added.

"Search me," said Sean. "All I know is that Michael is going to be here soon. Really soon!" His mother rubbed her swollen belly. She was due to have the baby in about six weeks.

"I sure am glad that Michael's mother will be here before the baby is born to help me with it," she said. "And now I have to start our plans for a welcome party when they arrive."

"I can help you get ready for the party if you want me to," Sean added.

"I would like that," she said. Sean's mother always felt bad that her son had not made many friends in the neighborhood. It seemed that the melting pot of nationalities didn't always blend together. The different groups stayed to themselves and were wary of folks from different backgrounds. Many of the other Irish who settled in Norristown were not in the neighborhood where Sean and his family lived, so he truly was on his own.

Sean looked at his mother and smiled. "Michael is on his way!" He danced around the kitchen floor while his mother laughed at his silliness.

Chapter Twenty-Three

As Uncle Liam loaded the cart for another trip to Queenstown, Michael felt sad to be leaving him. With his father in America for so long, Michael had grown quite attached to his uncle. "I am going to miss you," Michael said.

"And I, you," replied Uncle Liam. "But it won't be for long!"

"What do you mean?" questioned his nephew.

"Well, I just sent a letter off to your aunt and uncle and Sean. I posted it about two days ago back home. I figured it would reach America not too long after you will, and I wanted to surprise ya, but I may as well tell ya now. I am planning on going to America in the next month or two, and then I will be movin' the whole brood there eventually." He smiled at his nephew.

"That's great!" said Michael. This news really made Michael a little less homesick already knowing that the family would soon be together again in America. Eventually, the cart was loaded, the goodbyes were said, and they started out on their journey to Queenstown. Michael waved back at his aunt and cousins who stood along the village route as they departed.

Michael got his first view of the Titanic anchored in almost the same spot that Sean's Lusitania had occupied two years ago. The ship looked so beautiful to him, and all the people of Queenstown where chatting about this wonderful new liner on its maiden voyage to America.

His family boarded the tender, which soon chugged its way through the waters to the Titanic, which was moored in the harbor. Mailbags were brought on board the tender as well. Little did Michael and Uncle Liam know, but the letter Uncle Liam had written to Sean's family was also making the trip on the Titanic! As they moved along, he was listening to everyone's conversations about this wonderful liner.

"She is 882 feet long."

"She can hold 2200 passengers."

"I hear there are electric lights in every room and a heated swimming pool."
"There is a library on board too."
"And elevators!"

And there were many other things that he still did not know about the ship. The Marconi wireless radio had a daytime range of 400 miles and a nighttime range of 1,200 miles. The ship was carrying 43 tons of fresh meat, 40 tons of potatoes, 1,250 quarts of ice cream, 3 tons of butter, and over 1,200 gallons of milk. No, Michael was not aware of any of this. All he knew was that the ship was huge. No wonder they named her Titanic. She truly was titanic! He stared at her in awe.

Titanic's keel had been laid in 1909 and was launched in 1911. Built at the Harland and Wolff Shipyards in Belfast, Ireland, the Titanic was 90 feet longer than the Lusitania. Michael could not take his eyes off of this magnificent steamer. This ship was the most wonderful, the most spectacular, the most amazing thing he had ever seen.

"I hear she can go 21 knots," said another passenger. Michael snapped out of his Titanic trance.

The little tender continued churning its way towards the liner, and the ship seemed to grow in size the closer they got to it. "Isn't she grand!" said Michael's mother. Kathleen stared at the smokestacks.

"Mommy, it is so big!" Kathleen said. She held he mother's hand tightly.

"I think this is truly a wonderful ship!" Michael said out loud.

"And it is unsinkable too," said a man standing nearby. "She was built with 16 watertight compartments, and if any of them got ripped open she would still float."

"See those smokestacks?" said a man on the tender.

"Aye," said Michael.

"They are so big, a train could fit through them!"

"Wow!" was all Michael could say as the tender pulled up alongside the Titanic.

Eventually all the passengers and luggage were taken aboard. The mighty whistle was blown announcing the ship was about to continue its maiden voyage. The tender chugged back towards Queenstown. Many people stood out on the deck as the Titanic's propellers began to churn the waters. It was just two years ago when he was on the dock looking out at another ship that had taken his cousin away, and now he was about to join him in a new land. This was all so exciting to Michael. "Sean, here I come," he whispered to himself.

"Did ya hear 'bout what happened to the Titanic when she set sail in Southampton?" said a passenger. "It's a bad omen I tell ya."

Michael, Kathleen, and his mother turned to face the stranger as he told his story. "The Titanic almost hit another ship when she departed from England. She just missed the other ship by inches. This ship is doomed," he warned.

"Please sir," Michael's mother said, "you are scaring the children." He looked down at little Kathleen who did look a bit nervous. Kathleen squeezed her mother's hand a bit tighter.

"Oh, I am sure it is all right now, but it was scary there for a few seconds," he smiled as he looked down at the little girl. Then he added, "And of course, what could sink this ship? She is unsinkable!" He smiled, tipped his hat, and walked off.

"That's right, Mom," Michael began. "They say that the Titanic can not sink. Even God himself could not sink this ship!" said Michael, repeating one of the earlier comments he had heard.

"Michael, don't be so disrespectful to God!" his mother said. "I think we should go below now and get unpacked."

"Sorry, Mom," he said. They stood on deck a little longer. Michael and his sister and mother went below to check out the steerage accommodations after the sight of Ireland had disappeared over the horizon.

"Farewell, Ireland," Michael said.

The third class areas of the Titanic were deep in the bow and stern of the ship. These passengers were not permitted into second or first class areas, and many places were separated with locked gates to keep passengers where they belonged. The third class passengers had nothing to complain about. The rooms were all quite nice, and often even nicer than what most of them left behind at home. Michael was sure that he could still smell the paint. It was that fresh!

In some cases, the passengers in third class were not that concerned about their accommodations anyway. They had used their life savings and sold their homes and other prized possessions just to get a ticket on the Titanic. Their goal was to get to America, and Titanic was just the icing on the cake to get them there.

Michael was not only excited about going to America, but he also was excited about being on the largest and grandest ship in the world. He was going to explore this ship from bottom to top. And no one was going to stop him.

Chapter Twenty-Four

Sean was so excited that he would be seeing his best friend in just a few days. He even asked his mom if he could stay home from school, but of course she said that he could not. Still, it was such a thrilling time for the Monaghan family. The rest of the O'Brien's were coming to America, and Sean's mother would be having the baby anytime now. Sean gathered his books and went out the front door, whistling all the way down the street.

As Sean walked to school, he passed the stream that would become the new place to play when Michael got here. Then he remembered that snake he had seen recently. "I can't wait to show Michael a snake," he said to himself. He will think those opossums are funny looking animals too. I have so much to show him when he gets here." Sean picked up the pace so he would not be late for school.

All the children hung up their belongings in the cloak closet and then took their seats. The teacher started the day with the math lesson and then went into geography. Today's lesson was about the oceans of the world. Sean did not volunteer very often in school, but today he was so ecstatic about his cousin coming to town that he had his hand raised before he realized it.

"Yes, Sean," said the teacher.

"My cousin happens to be in the Atlantic Ocean right now," he said.

"In it?" one of the children said. "What is he, a fish?" All the other children laughed.

"Class, class, that's enough," chimed in the teacher as he gestured with his hands for silence. "Go ahead, Sean."

Sean continued, "He is on the Titanic and coming to Norristown to live with his dad, so he is in the Atlantic Ocean."

"On," corrected the teacher. "He is in a ship that is on the ocean." Sean nodded that he understood. "Sean, that is wonderful that you have family coming to join you in America." Sean beamed from ear to ear.

Then the conversation turned briefly to the Titanic, and it was time for lunch.

"You made that up about your cousin," said one of the kids at the lunch table. "He ain't on the Titanic."

"No I did not make it up!" said Sean.

"We don't believe you at all."

"You will see!" said Sean. "Why would I say it if it weren't true?"

"You just wanted the teacher's attention," said another classmate.

Sean could feel his face getting red with anger. He thought to himself, "These kids. I hate them. I don't care if they believe me or not. They will see when I walk to school with Michael next week." He could feel tears of anger well up in his eyes, but he dare not cry at school, or the other kids would have a heyday with that.

Sean could barely finish eating his lunch. These kids had been mean to him since he moved here. At that moment he realized that he missed his cousin more than ever. Even Kathleen would be better to play with than these children. "Michael, please get here as fast as you can," Sean said to himself.

He stared out the window thinking of his cousin. He quietly said to himself, "Friends forever we will be."

And once Michael even got all the way upstairs into the first class areas.

Chapter Twenty-Five

Michael leaned over the railing, staring at the water below. "I still can't believe I am finally going to America. The land of opportunity! I never thought this day would come. I can't wait to see Dad again, and Sean," he thought to himself as he watched the wake that the ship's path made in the water. "And I am getting to America on the grandest ship ever built," he added.

Michael had really been enjoying the maiden voyage of the Titanic. He thought the food was quite good, and during the day he spent time on deck talking with other teenagers or sneaking into areas of the ship that were off limits to third class passengers. He successfully made it up to second class three times, and once he even got all the way upstairs into the first class areas. He had just poked his head into the first class dining room when a crewmember spotted him, and he took off back to the security of the steerage areas of the ship.

And what opulence he would have witnessed had he been able to poke his head around a bit longer in first class. Almost 700 of the 2400 passengers on the Titanic were traveling in first class style. They had dining rooms, lounges, reading and writing rooms, verandah cafés and squash courts.

First class even had Turkish baths and a swimming pool. The gymnasium had rowing machines and mechanical camels to ride. Of course, first class passengers traveled with their maids and butlers and valets, so they were well taken care of. It truly was a classy way to travel. Even their dogs were groomed and cared for in first class kennels!

And far below so much work was going on to make this journey an enjoyable one for Michael and all of the passengers. On one deck the kitchen crew was busily preparing the next meal. On another deck, the postal workers were busily sorting the mail so that when the Titanic docked in New York, it would be ready to continue its journey according to its delivery destination. Uncle Liam's letter had been placed with all the Philadelphia, Pennsylvania mail. Far below, the stokers tended to the coal fires to keep the Titanic moving at its present pace towards Michael's new home.

This past morning, Michael and his mother had gone to the church service, and the rest of the day was like a relaxing Sunday back home in Ireland. He thought about his Uncle Liam and other family members back home in the village. Michael already missed all the seabirds that lived in his lowland island home. He wondered what birds lived in America. Then he thought about Sean and his father. He smiled and announced to himself, "I am definitely heading in the right direction." It had been a very long day, and everyone had turned in early that night.

Around 11:30, there was a slight grinding noise. Michael awoke as did his mother. "What was that?" she asked.

"Oh, someone must have fallen out of their bed next to us," Michael laughed. They lay still in the darkness, but could hear some commotion from somewhere else in third class. Then the Titanic's engines stopped. Michael sat up. His mother jumped out of her bed and turned on the lights.

"I don't like this one bit," she said. "This can't be good." Michael was already out of bed and putting on his clothes.

As he pulled on his boots, he said, "Let me go find out what is going on. You stay here with Kathleen." His worried mother nodded and opened the door for him.

Michael was not gone very long when he returned to the room. He looked very upset. "What is it?" his mother asked. Kathleen sighed and rolled over in her bed.

"They say the Titanic lost a propeller. We may have to go back."

"Oh dear," his mother said as she wrung her hands together.

"It looks like I will never make it to America," Michael added.

Just then there was a knock at the door. A steward was telling everyone to put on the lifejackets.

"What?" gasped Mrs. O'Brien. "There must be something going on a whole lot worse than a missing propeller!" She got up and started to dress. "Wake up your sister and help her dress. I will start to pack up our things. We better do what we are told." Michael shook Kathleen awake and helped the groggy child to dress.

Soon the three O'Briens were in the corridor with their luggage heading for the stairs. The lifejackets were so constricting, and little Kathleen complained that it hurt her.

"You can't take your luggage!" said one of the stewards.

"But this is everything we have in the world," said Michael's mother.

"Sorry madam, but orders from the captain. You are to wait here until third class is told to move."

"Wait here?" exclaimed the man from the cabin next to theirs. "They are going to drown us like rats. I hear that there is already water coming in up front, and they want us to wait here?" The man ran off.

"Water?" gasped Michael's mother. "Michael, what are we going to do?" she pleaded.

Michael looked around at all the panicked faces, and he knew that things could get out of hand. He realized that many of these passengers could not even speak English and had no idea what was happening. "Follow me," he said. Michael's mother grabbed Kathleen's hand and obeyed.

Michael was able to trace his path that he had taken the last few nights when he had been secretly exploring the upper decks of the Titanic. He led his family up and down various stairwells and in and out of hallways like he was the captain of the ship himself. "How do ya know all this?" said his mother.

Michael smiled and said, "Uh, just instinct, I guess." Soon the trio was safely on the upper deck of the ship where the lifeboats were, and to their amazement they were being loaded. "What about all those people down below?" he said. His mother just stared out into the dark starlit sky above the Atlantic Ocean. They could feel a slight tilt of the deck under their feet.

"Mommy, I'm cold!" complained Kathleen. At that moment, the band started to play music.

"It can't be that bad if they are entertaining us," said Michael's mother. But Michael was not so sure about that.

"You two stay here. I am going to find out what lifeboat they want us to get into." His mother nodded her head to show she understood. She was never more proud of her son than she was right now, seeing him take charge of his family so bravely. She had not realized until this moment that her little boy had grown into a fine young man.

Michael approached a group of crewmembers preparing a lifeboat for lowering when he overheard their conversation.

"Iceberg ripped us open like a tin opener!" said one of the sailors.

"And they say there are not enough lifeboats for the men!"

Michael froze in place, trying to grasp what he had heard.

"An iceberg? But the Titanic is unsinkable. Surely we must be okay," he said to himself. He stood and watched the crew prepare the lifeboat. "Excuse me. Can I bring my family here to get in this boat when it is ready?"

"Sure, kid, but you better hurry. We may be eating sand for supper tonight!" Michael gasped, nodded, and then ran off to fetch his mother and sister. They had waited just where they had been told to wait.

"Come on. I have a lifeboat for you," he ordered. "Please hurry!"

"Don't you mean us?" his mother said. Michael smiled and nodded and took his sister by the hand and asked them to follow him. Soon they had fought through the growing crowds of passengers and made it to the lifeboat that was now almost full.

"Excuse me, sir, here is my family," Michael said. He gave his mother a big hug good-bye. His mother took the crewman's hand as he helped her into the lifeboat. Michael looked at his sister and said, "You know, for a sister, you are okay." He smiled at her, and she returned the smile back to him. Then he grabbed Kathleen and hoisted her into the boat. She sat down next to her mother.

"Come on now, Michael, get in," his mother ordered.

"It's women and children only, miss," said one of the sailors.

"But he is a child," she pleaded.

"Mom, I am sixteen now," Michael corrected. The sailor looked at Michael and smiled.

"Aye, he is a man now, madam," he added.

"Don't worry about me, Mom," said Michael. "There are plenty of other boats. I will get one of those." He knew better, but he bravely smiled and waved as the lifeboat began its drop into the icy cold Atlantic below. "I will see you soon," he shouted to them as they disappeared from sight.

"That's a mighty fine thing ya did for yer mom and sister," the sailor said as he continued to lower the lifeboat with the ropes. Far below deck, the crew continued to keep the power on so that the lights would not fail and the passengers would remain calm. The postal workers moved the heavy sacks of mail up the steps to a drier deck. They worked diligently to save the mail from the rising waters.

Once the lifeboat was lowered into the water, Michael watched it until it disappeared into the darkness. Then he just stood there. Alone. The Titanic continued its tilt forward. Michael, like the rest of the crowd, instinctively moved toward the stern of the ship as the tilt worsened. The ship groaned and moaned as it was put to its greatest tests of endurance.

Meanwhile, Kathleen and her mother floated into the darkness, worrying about Michael and hoping that he was in another lifeboat by now. They could hear the Titanic being put to its tests of strength. Michael's mother thought back to the passenger who had made the comment that this ship was doomed. She wondered if he made it into the same lifeboat with her son.

By 1:30, Michael was sure that there truly was no hope for the Titanic. He knew it was really going to founder. Water was pouring over the bow of the ship. He watched some men trying to tie deck chairs together in an effort to make a raft.

"Every man for himself!" came a cry from somewhere else in the ship. The band continued to play music.

By 2:20, the Titanic had met its match. The lights went out. The ship was almost bobbing perpendicular to the water. The din created by the ship in its precarious position was unbelievable as everything below crashed towards the submerged bow of the ship. Tons of coal. Twenty-nine boilers. White Star Line China. Chairs. Tables. Five pianos. Luggage in storage. 20,000 bottles of beer. 1,000 oyster forks. 12,000 dinner plates. 6,000 table cloths. 500 salad bowls.

And Uncle Liam's letter.

The lights flickered off, came back on, and then went out again forever. The forward funnel toppled over to the seabed below, smashing passengers who unluckily were swimming in its path. Passengers on board continued to scream for help.

Michael tried to hang on as the Titanic began its death plunge into the icy water. The ship went down so quickly. Passengers in the nearby lifeboats watched this horrific scene. With just a quiet gulping sound, the Titanic was gone, and then the worst sounds of all could be heard by those persons seated in the lifeboats: the sounds of hundreds of people crying to be saved. Kathleen began to cry as her mother tried to comfort her.

For a little while, Michael tried to swim in the icy cold, trying to find a lifeboat. Someone swam near him and pushed him down, but he fought his way free and swam slowly away. Soon his limbs grew weaker and weaker. "I am so cold. So cold," he said. He was getting sleepy. Very sleepy. He could barely feel his arms and legs anymore. He thought of Ireland, his mom and Kathleen, and his father. He felt groggy. Confused. Cold. He had one final thought, and that was of Sean.

* * *

Sean sat bolt upright in bed. He was breathing hard. He was soaked with perspiration. He could not remember the details of the dream he just had, but Michael was in the dream, and he was in trouble. "I hate dreams like that," Sean said as he yawned and tried to snuggle back under his sheets. It was 2:45 in the morning when the dream occurred.

* * *

Michael's still body drifted amongst the bodies of 1500 other souls lost the night of April 15, 1912. It was 2:45 in the morning.

Once the lifeboat was lowered into the water,
Michael watched it until it disappeared into the darkness.

Chapter Twenty-Six

Sean woke up rather late the next morning. For a few minutes he laid there gathering his thoughts. He yawned and stretched. Just then, he thought he heard crying downstairs. He listened more closely. Someone *was* crying. He quickly put on his clothes and went downstairs to find out what was going on. As he bounded down the steps, he saw his father comforting his mother. Her face was buried in a handkerchief. "What is wrong?" he asked.

"Son, I have some terrible news," started his father. "The Titanic has hit an iceberg and sunk." Sean's mother began to sob more.

"What?" Sean said. "But Michael wrote in his letter that the ship was unsinkable. Everyone said that the ship was unsinkable!" Then he stopped talking. He looked at his father and said, "Is Michael okay?"

"We don't know. Your Uncle Patrick heard about the news when he showed up for work at the *Herald* this morning. He has gone to New York to meet the Carpathia. That is the ship which has picked up the survivors. We sure hope everyone is okay. Pray son. Pray really hard."

The rest of the day and most of the week passed quietly and slowly with no word from the family. The Norristown and Philadelphia newspapers were filled with headline news about the Titanic, and the news did not look good. It was almost as if the newsprint was screaming out the horrible words: "Over 1500 persons perished in the Titanic disaster. Most of the lifeboats left the sinking ship with extra seats available. Only 705 survivors were rescued and will soon reach New York Harbor on the Carpathia."

Days passed until Uncle Patrick returned home. It was Sean who first spotted the wagon coming up the street. "They are here! They are here!" Sean shouted. The Monaghans ran out the door to greet them. Sean's mother still looked so worried, and Sean could see his uncle and aunt sitting on the seat next to him, so he assumed the children were in the back." Sean thought it was odd that Michael would not be standing in the back waving at him with excitement. He strained his eyes to take a closer look.

"I guess he is exhausted from the disaster," Sean thought to himself. "He must be resting in the back."

The wagon came to a halt, and the Monaghans quickly crossed the street. They could see the shock on their faces and their overwhelming sadness, as only Kathleen sat up from the back of the wagon. Sean's eyes grew wide. His mouth dropped open. Some of the neighbors came out into the street.

Michael's mother began to cry. "We lost our little boy," she cried. Sean's mother began to cry again, and Sean just stood there in total disbelief.

"No, no, no! It can't be true!" Then he turned and ran back to his bedroom, and stared at the picture of his cousin on the wall in disbelief. He found himself crying harder than he ever cried before. They were tears of sadness. Titanic tears. And Sean cried for a very long time.

It was a week later that a memorial service was held for Michael. It was nothing elaborate, but it was a nice tribute to Sean's cousin. The priest talked of Michael's bravery on the Titanic and how he saved his mother and Kathleen from death. Sean found the words comforting, yet he still knew that he would never see his cousin again, and this caused him great pain. His best friend in the world was gone. He would never see Michael again.

"No matter how long the day, the evening will come," said the priest softly. "The pain and loss you feel now will lessen, but there will always be an empty spot in your hearts for young Michael. What you need to do is store your wonderful memories of this brave lad in that spot and always hold him near to you through these thoughts."

At the end of the service, the congregation joined the family to sing the Irish song, Danny Boy.

> Oh Danny boy, the pipes, the pipes are calling
> From glen to glen, and down the mountain side
> The summer's gone, and all the flowers are dying
> 'tis you, 'tis you must go and I must bide.
>
> But come ye back when summer's in the meadow
> Or when the valley's hushed and white with snow
> 'tis I'll be here in sunshine or in shadow
> Oh Danny boy, oh Danny boy, I love you so.

And if you come, when all the flowers are dying
And I am dead, as dead I well may be
You'll come and find the place where I am lying
And kneel and say an "Ave" there for me.

And I shall hear, tho' soft you tread above me
And all my dreams will warm and sweeter be
If you'll not fail to tell me that you love me
I'll simply sleep in peace until you come to me.

I'll simply sleep in peace until you come to me.

Sean wiped one more tear from his eye as they left the church and headed back home, and his heart was empty that day.

Michael O'Brien
1896-1912

Epilogue

Several weeks after the disaster, a letter arrived from Ireland. It was from Uncle Liam expressing his sympathy. In the letter he told his family in America that they would be pleased to know that Michael had not been forgotten, and a service was held in the village church in his honor. In fact, the service was well attended. Uncle Liam also told them that two families in nearby villages had also lost family members on the Titanic, and all of Ireland was grieving for their loss. At the close of the letter, he mentioned once again that he would soon be leaving for Norristown, having no idea that his original letter about this now lay deep at the bottom of the ocean.

Three weeks later, Sean's little brother was born. Although his birth did not remove the sadness of the devastating loss from the O'Brien and Monaghan households, it helped mend the emptiness and sorrow they were all feeling.

Sean's parents decided to name their new son Michael, which was a great tribute to their wonderful nephew, and it seemed to please Uncle Patrick and his wife very much.

Sean went in to the baby's room one day, and looked down at his little brother. He put his finger into the hand of little Michael, and his new baby brother grabbed it. Sean thought to himself, "You are going to be strong. Just like your big cousin was." Then he sat on the chair next to his new brother and said, "You and I are going to be good friends."

He added,

> "Here's to you, and here's to me.
> Friends forever we will be.
> And if we should ever disagree,
> Then heck with you, and here's to me!"

And his little brother gurgled up at him and smiled.

Conclusion

Scattered icebergs and grinding ice floes continued their way through the ocean, helping to maintain the frigid temperatures at sea.

According to the official report, 1513 persons died as a result of the Titanic sinking; only 711 in all were saved. Of the 706 third class passengers, 528 lost their lives that evening—a far higher percentage than for second or first class passengers.

Three boats from Nova Scotia and one from Newfoundland sailed back and forth across the area, looking for bodies to take back to Halifax for identification and a suitable burial. The task was very hard and very sad. Floating ice would scrape along the sides of these ships as they continued their task.

Only 335 bodies were ever found, among them multi-millionaire John Jacob Astor, bandleader Wallace Hartley, and two children. The crewmembers cried as these youngest victims were brought on board the search vessels.

120 of the passengers on the Titanic came from Ireland, paying between three and eight pounds for the voyage that promised to take them to a better life. Most of them never made it, instead losing their lives to the icy ocean.

Of the 113 passengers who boarded at Queenstown, 74 died at sea.

The efforts to locate victims continued for over a month.

Michael's body was never found.

Acknowledgments

We would like to thank the following people for their input, help, ideas, and support.

First, a big thank you to Kilian Harford from the Irish Titanic Historical Society, as well as his wife Mary, who helped keep our Irish facts straight.

A thank you to Curt Morelock, author of *Warp Factor II: Titanic II* and *Event 2012*, for his support.

Thank you to Kyrila Scully, author of *Titanic: The Survivors*, for those encouraging words!

Thank you to Diana Bristow, author of *Californian and Titanic: Facts vs. Myths, Titanic: Sinking the Myths, Titanic Calling, Captain's Karma*, and *Titanic R.I.P. Can Dead Men Tell Tales*, for her support and emails.

Thanks to Charles Haas, co-author of *Titanic: Triumph and Tragedy, Falling Star, Titanic: Destination Disaster*, and *Titanic: A Journey Through Time* for his ideas and suggestions.

Our gratitude goes to a variety of Internet Sites that make available pictures that are in the public domain. This especially includes Public Domain Photos, at pdphoto.org, for the picture of Ireland we include on the cover. Also, thanks go to the marvelous Archival Research Catalog, provided online by the National Archives at http://www.archives.gov/research/arc/ as well as the Library of Congress site http://lcweb2.loc.gov/pp/mdbquery.html.

The picture of the Titanic on the cover is the last picture taken of the ship as she left Queenstown. This copyrighted photo has been used in cooperation with the Father Browne Collection.

Of course, we also thank all of those individuals and organizations worldwide that have kept the story of the Titanic alive, through their books, newsletters, publications, and undying interest in this historic ship.

And finally, thanks to all our family and friends for their encouragement.